THE CHURCH MICE ADRIFT

A TEMPLAR BOOK

This edition published in the UK in 2010 by Templar Publishing,
an imprint of The Templar Company Limited,
The Granary, North Street, Dorking, Surrey, RH4 1DN, UK
www.templarco.co.uk

First published in the UK in 1976 by Macmillan

ISBN 978-1-84877-062-1

Printed in China

THE
CHURCH MICE
ADRIFT

GRAHAM OAKLEY

templar publishing

MODERN CLASSICS

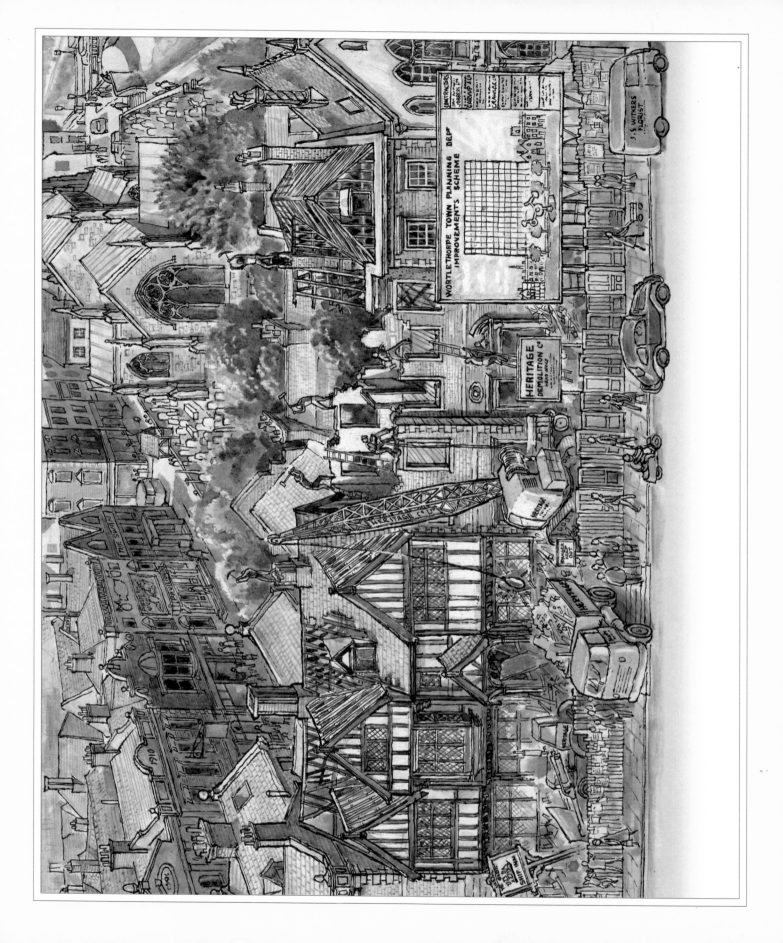

IT HAD BEEN decided in the Town Hall that Wortlethorpe must keep up with the times, and so great changes were starting to take place.

There were some who thought this was a very good thing...

Because, for some, finding a new home isn't that easy...

and there were some who didn't.

and they have to search far and wide,
and look in the most unusual places…

and when at last they have found one, it is usually full
of little inconveniences that have to be sorted out.

The church mice were having a nice chat about cats and, as Sampson the church cat was out for the evening, they were being very rude about them, particularly ginger ones, when suddenly...

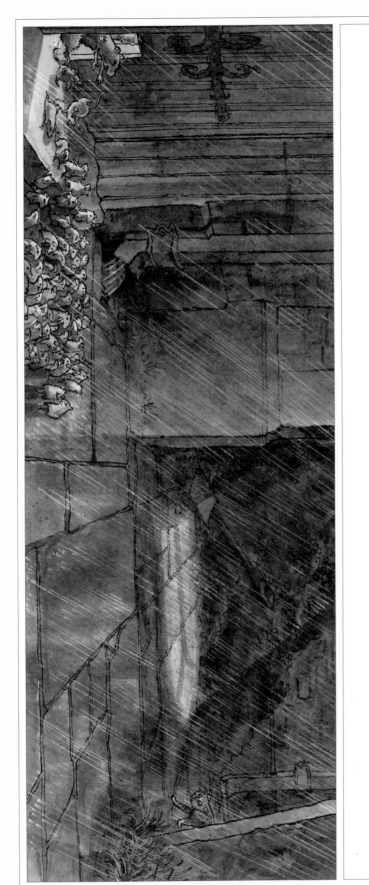

their whole world collapsed about their ears.

Just stand well back and watch me."

It was a dismal sight that greeted Sampson's eyes when he
arrived home. But after listening to the mice's sad tale
he decided that things weren't as bad as they looked.
"Don't worry, chaps," he said. "A lightning pounce,
a few quick one-twos with the old paws,
and your troubles will be over…

So they stood well back and watched him...

but what they saw was not entirely cheering.

At length, Sampson mumbled dejectedly that he knew a place to shelter if they cared to follow him, and being fed up with rain, wind and poetry, the mice followed. Humphrey said that he wasn't accustomed to following paper tigers, or rather completely useless cats, but the next gust of wind and rain changed his mind about all that.

It was a wet night in the churchyard.

Arthur and Humphrey tried to hearten everybody by reciting poems about straight backs, unbending knees and stiff upper lips, but it was cold comfort.

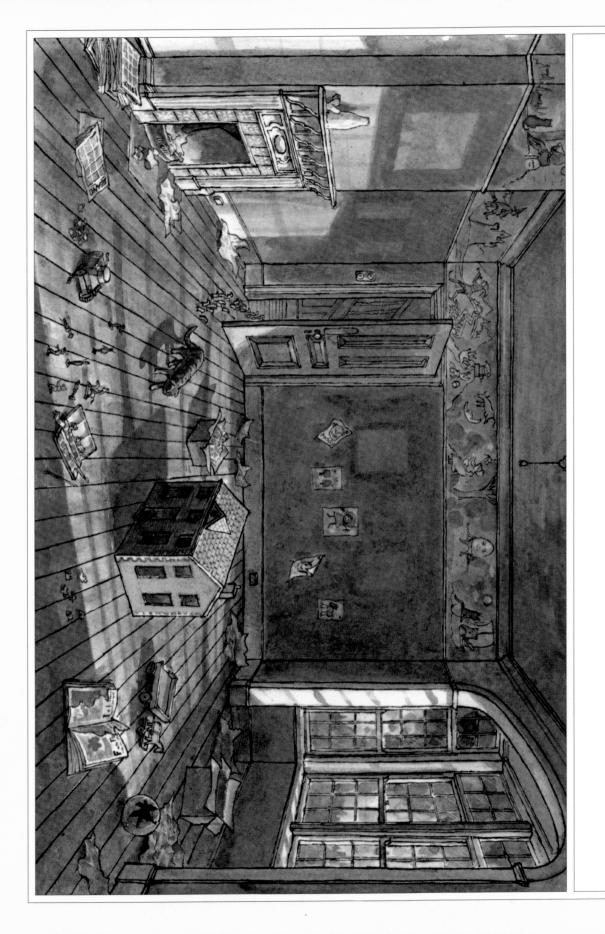

Sampson led them to an empty house.

It was damp and cold but much better than the churchyard.

They chose the most cheerful and least draughty room and grumbled themselves to sleep.

Next morning, Humphrey called an emergency meeting.

He said that it was no use relying on a certain so-called cat for help. The finger of destiny had beckoned *him* to lead the mice in triumph back to their native vestry; his sword wouldn't rest in his hand until feet had trampled the rats into the dust, and British mice never, never, never would be slaves.

Then Arthur stood up.

That kind of stuff was all very well, he said, but what was needed was an *intelligent* plan, and he had one. The mice must be welded into a ruthless fighting machine. He had nothing to offer them but blood, sweat and tears, and two jelly beans each once they got back to the vestry. Strict military training was to start at once, with no shirking.

Arthur, Humphrey and one or two others who were clued up in military matters directed operations.

Sampson watched for a while, and what he saw only confirmed his opinion that if the rats were to be thrown out of the vestry, they'd have to leave it to him.

"What I do for those mice," he sighed as he strolled out to think up a plan, but deep down he knew it was really his own reputation he had to do something for.

And it was pure chance that the first thing he saw on returning to the mice was the abandoned dolls' house.

But it was pure genius that made him put all the chances together into a brilliant plan.

And it was pure chance that having got them and eaten them, he went down to the riverbank to digest them.

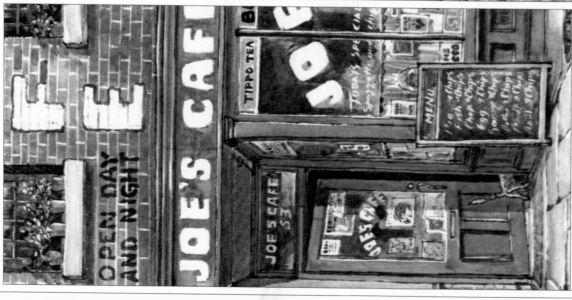

It was pure chance that at that moment he felt like some juicy bacon rinds and went where he could get them.

When he had got the mice together and explained his plan, they admitted it was not bad considering he was only a cat. Anyway, everybody was sick of being soldiers. So Sampson (who was good at scavenging) was put in charge of finding provisions, and Arthur (who was practical) was put in charge of construction, and Humphrey (who was not very good at anything) was put in charge of the artistic side of things.

Arthur and Humphrey and their forces set about their tasks at once...

Sampson and his team went out and set about theirs...

and when all was ready, they took everything down to the riverbank.

The dolls' house floated beautifully, and they tied it to the bank while they went to work, inside and out.

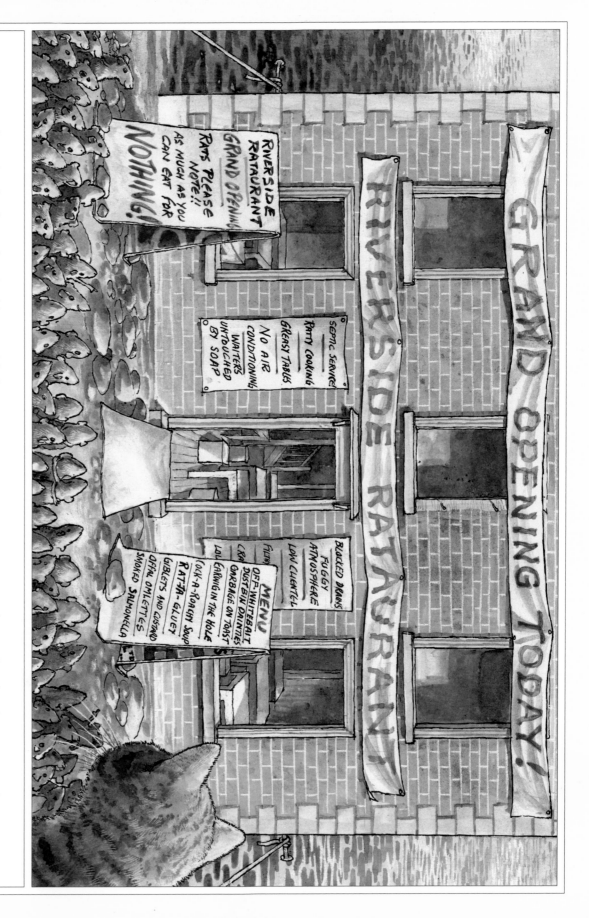

When the final touches had been added, everybody stood back to admire their handiwork.

Then the mice with the loudest voices were sent off to shout, "Free grub for all rats!" outside the vestry, and while they were gone,

straws were drawn for the dangerous job of serving in the café. The losers reluctantly went aboard. Humphrey and Arthur were unanimously voted head waiters.

Everyone else concealed themselves on the bank.

They were really feeling quite hungry because it was at least ten minutes since they'd finished their seventeen-course breakfast in the vestry.

This was hardly done before the rats arrived.

After the thirty-fourth helping, the rats felt a bit better and ready for a little after-dinner revelry. This was the opportunity the waiters had been waiting for. They quietly crept ashore, and if

Humphrey hadn't chosen that moment to improve the rats' minds with a lecture on *Etiquette in the Court of Louis XIV*, and Arthur hadn't waited for him, they too might have escaped.

As soon as the dolls' house started to move,
four things happened. Firstly, the rats saw they
had been tricked and fell into a dreadful rage.
Secondly, Arthur and Humphrey realised
the awful danger they were in.

But in the excitement no one had thought
to count the waiters as they came ashore.
When the dolls' house was set adrift,
Arthur and Humphrey were still inside.

Thirdly, Sampson and all the mice ashore saw
that a terrible mistake had been made.

Fourthly, the rats found they had someone
to vent their dreadful rage on.

But before you vent your rage on somebody you have to catch them...

and Arthur and Humphrey proved to be pretty slippery customers when it was a question of life and limb.

Moreover, a snack of thirty-four helpings on top of a seventeen-course breakfast doesn't improve a rat's nimbleness. And then the mice had a trick or two up their sleeves, which gained them a breather.

The house was drifting faster and faster.
If Arthur and Humphrey were to be rescued,
it must be now or never. Sampson saw his chance,
and quick as a flash he took it.

But dolls' houses are not large,
and soon there was nowhere else to run to.

He made all the mice who could climb follow him...

because he needed a little extra weight...

to do what had to be done.

Their timing was absolutely...

perfect.

Suddenly, without any warning, they experienced a down, which kept on going down...

However, life is a series of ups and downs.

and down and down, until it looked as though there would
be no more *ups* for them, when…

in a flash, they were saved.
All had ended happily, at least for the mice...

but for Sampson the worst was yet to come.

He told himself that this was the price a chap paid for being irresistible, but it didn't help.

They had left the vestry in a disgusting state. It took four days of hard work to make it fit for decent mice to live in. But when several weeks had passed and the rats had not returned, the mice knew they were safe and gave a party to celebrate. It lasted all night, and even Sampson enjoyed it, because it took his mind off things like asking himself over and over again what other hero, in the moment of his triumph, had been picked up, turned over and tickled in public?

He never found an answer, and it was a long, long time before the mice could stop him diving under the surplice cupboard every time he heard a lady's footsteps outside the vestry.

They were taken all the way back to the vestry, and before she left, the lady said she would visit Sampson frequently and she promised to bring him a nice red collar with a bell on it.

The thought put him off his food for weeks.

The rats came to a very sticky end, though not in the usual sense. The dolls' house ran aground at the Wortlethorpe Bone & Fish Glue Company's factory, and the sights and perfumes there were more beautiful than anything the rats had ever dreamed of. They forgot all about the mice and Sampson, and lived happily ever after.

THE END

GRAHAM OAKLEY

AND THE CHURCH MICE SERIES

When Graham Oakley began THE CHURCH MOUSE, he intended to create a series of stories about different public buildings in Wortlethorpe, but the first book was so successful that he never got on to the library!

Instead, the stories of Sampson and the church mice became modern children's classics, garnering critical acclaim and capturing the imagination of a generation of children.

Between 1972 and 2000, Graham wrote and illustrated fourteen CHURCH MICE tales. The series was nominated for two Kate Greenaway Medals, won a *New York Times* Best Illustrated Children's Book award and sold over one and a half million books worldwide.